CLASS PET SQUAD

Journey to the
Center of Town

DAN YACCARINO

FEIWEL AND FRIENDS
NEW YORK

A Feiwel and Friends Book
An Imprint of Macmillan

Our books may be purchased in bulk for promotional, educational, or business use.
Please contact your local bookseller or the Macmillan Corporate and Premium Sales Department
at (800) 221-7945 ext. 5442 or by e-mail at MacmillanSpecialMarkets@macmillan.com.

Library of Congress Cataloging-in-Publication Data Available
ISBN: 978-1-250-02462-6 (hardcover) / 978-1-250-08676-1 (ebook)

Book design by Patrick Collins

Feiwel and Friends logo designed by Filomena Tuosto

First Edition: 2016

10 9 8 7 6 5 4 3 2 1

mackids.com

For Sunny Tiger

WeLCoMe TO
PUbLIC SchOOL
1000

INTRODUCTION

Every school needs a little help now and then, especially PS 1000.

Sure, just like your school, PS 1000 has teachers, a principal, and the school's maintenance crew, who all keep everything running smoothly, *but they don't do it alone*!

Who do you think makes sure everyone gets back on the bus after a class trip? Who doesn't let the scenery in the school play accidentally fall over? Who fights off a gang of rampaging squirrels trying to steal chocolate pudding cups from the cafeteria for tomorrow's lunch?

The Class Pet Squad, *that's* who!

MEET THE
CLASS PET SQUAD!

MAX

He's the muscle of the Class Pet Squad and the big picture guy, er—*hamster*. He may look cute and cuddly, but make no mistake! He's tough as nails and there's nothing he wouldn't do for the kids of PS 1000.

RHONDA

She's the Squad's heart and go-to member for mapping out routes and locating supplies, but being a chameleon, she'll sometimes disappear when she gets scared.

JULIUS

He's the brains of the group who figures out the logistics of each mission and what the Squad will need, like helicopters, catapults, and lots of snacks in case they get hungry.

SUZU

Nobody's really sure what part of the Squad's body Suzu is or what she actually *does*. Especially Suzu, but she sure has fun doing it and it usually involves glitter. Lots and lots of glitter.

THE MAESTROS: HARRY, JOE, and SHIRLEY

These three mice are geniuses. Well, Joe and Shirley are. No one's quite sure about Harry. They build everything the Squad needs for their missions: submarines out of milk cartons, catapults out of rulers, grappling hooks from paper clips, and parachutes out of sandwich bags.

They even invented a cheese-fueled vehicle. Don't ask.

CHAPTER ONE

It was a typical day at PS 1000.

Max listened to the students give their Show and Tell presentations and learned all about sea shells, a bag of dead bugs, a bottle cap, and a marble Hoyt Schermerhorn claimed his little brother swallowed last week.

The final presentation was given by Ben McGillicutty. He stood in front of the class and held up his favorite toy, Sharkman.

Ben explained why, even though it had some teeth marks on it from his dog Brutus, Sharkman was the absolute best toy he's ever had, even better than his bike, the remote control car that his mother still wouldn't let him play with ever since he broke the lamp with it—even though it was an accident—or the rocket launcher his uncle got him that his father said he could play with when he got a little older.

Then he told the story about how while on a
family road trip, he accidentally left Sharkman at
a rest stop, but only realized it after they'd been

driving for an hour. His father drove all the way back
to get him.

Sharkman had not been on vacation since.

One of the kids asked *why* he was the best toy he ever had.

"Because he's *cool*," Ben replied.

The class nodded in agreement. Sharkman *was* pretty cool.

"Every night before I go to bed," Ben explained as the toy was passed around, "I line up all of my action figures on the shelf in my room."

Another kid raised a hand and asked why he did that.

"I won't be able to sleep unless they're all there," Ben explained.

Max stopped running on his wheel.

He understood how important Sharkman was to Ben. Max wanted everything in order before bunking down for the night, too. Max's running wheel needed to be oiled, his water bottle needed to be filled, and his favorite toy needed to be in its proper place.

Just then, the last bell rang and the day was over for the students, but Max's had just begun.

CHAPTER TWO

The classrooms were empty and quiet. The students, teachers, and maintenance crew were finally gone for the day. It was time for Max to make his usual rounds, checking that the classrooms were in tip-top shape.

The last thing he did before moving on to cafeteria inspection was check the cubbies.

As Max marched up to the wall of cubbies,

he saw something. He climbed up and peeked.

It was Sharkman!

Ben McGillicutty accidentally left Sharkman at school!

Then Max remembered that Ben couldn't fall

asleep unless Sharkman was lined up on his shelf
with the rest of his action figures.

Max knew what he had to do.

So, he sprang into action.

"What's a 'Code Red,' Max?" Suzu asked as she hopped into the room with Julius, Rhonda, and the Maestros a few seconds later.

"'Code Red' means an emergency situation!" Max explained. "I tell you that *every time*!"

"Well, why don't you just say *that*?" Suzu asked.

Max smacked his forehead and rolled his eyes. Then he climbed up on the teacher's desk as the rest gathered around.

"What's the emergency, Max?" Rhonda asked.

"This," Max replied as he held Sharkman up over his head.

"He's kind of scary looking," Rhonda shuddered.

Suzu thought he needed some glitter.

"This is Ben McGillicutty's favorite toy," Max announced. "And he can't get to sleep unless it's on the shelf in his room."

"So?" Julius asked.

"*So*?" Max spat. "So, this toy is going to be on that kid's shelf before he turns off his light *tonight*!"

"It would be quite impossible to get that toy all the way to Ben's house," Julius stated.

"And it would be awful scary to go outside after dark," said Rhonda.

"It would be fun!" Suzu squealed.

"We're going on an adventure! Yay!" Suzu cheered, hopping up and down. "Yippee!"

"This is *not* an adventure!" Max shouted. "It's a *dangerous mission*!"

Julius slowly scratched his head.

"Well, why couldn't he just bring it home *tomorrow*?" he asked.

"No student at PS 1000 is not going to get a full night's sleep when the Class Pet Squad is on the job!" Max said. "Not on *my* watch, anyway!"

Rhonda couldn't imagine losing something so important, like the green rock and plastic palm tree in her tank.

Julius understood that Ben needed all of his toys to be neatly lined up before going to sleep, so he tried to think of a way to solve this, like a puzzle or a math equation.

"Okay, everybody! Let's come up with a way to get Sharkman back to Ben McGillicutty!" Max ordered.

"I've *got* it!" Max shouted. "We're going to deliver it right to his bedroom and we're going to need a vehicle."

"Not to worry!" said Joe.

"We're on it!" said Shirley.

Harry nodded.

Julius paced back and forth saying *hmm*. They knew Julius was thinking, because he always paced and said *hmm* when he was thinking.

"This vehicle needs to be large enough for all of us, as well as Sharkman, but be something that no one will notice," Julius finally said.

"How will we do *that*?" asked Joe.

"That's *your* problem," Max said evenly.

Then Max doled out jobs to the rest of the Squad. Rhonda was to find Ben's address, print out a map of the neighborhood, and figure out the quickest route there. Julius was to make a list of everything they'd need both for the journey and to get them into Ben's bedroom. The Maestros were to help gather materials and build everything.

"Hey! What about *me*?" asked Suzu. "What do *I* do?"

"Just stay out of trouble!" replied Max.

CHAPTER THREE

Once Max made sure his team was on task, he climbed up to the windowsill and took a long look around the classroom. The seats were empty, but when the sun rose tomorrow morning they'd be filled with students. *His* students. And there was nothing he wouldn't do for each and every one of them.

Then he turned toward the window and as he watched the setting sun, he thought about Ben

McGillicutty. Max knew it was his duty to get Sharkman to him by bedtime.

"Hang on, kid," Max whispered. "The Class Pet Squad is on its way."

"Um, *Max*?" a voice said.

Max quickly brushed away a tear and turned to see Shirley looking up at him.

"Yes?" Max composed himself. "What is it?"

"We still need a part for the vehicle," she explained. "I think we're going to have to call, um, *them*."

"Are you *sure*?" Max asked. "Because you know I don't want to call those guys unless I absolutely *have* to."

Shirley said she was sure. They scoured the classrooms, the Lost and Found box, the supply closet, and even the cafeteria, but they couldn't find the one thing they needed to power the vehicle.

"We need a fishing-pole reel," she explained.

All the way up to the roof, Max shook his
head and muttered to himself as Shirley trailed
behind. Max climbed up to the mouth of a drainpipe

and asked Shirley one last time if she was
absolutely sure they really needed a fishing-pole
reel.

"I'm *sure*," Shirley said.

Max drew a heavy sigh.

"Second Street Specials!" he reluctantly shouted
into the drainpipe. "We need you!"

"Well, well, well, fellas," Ralph the Rat snickered to his gang as he sauntered up to Max. "It seems that our old friends the Class Pet Squad request our presence."

Shirley nervously hid behind Max.

"Don't worry, kid," Ralph said, smiling a toothy grin at her. "I don't bite."

Max glowered at Ralph, keeping a careful eye on him.

"Now, why would the squeaky clean heroes of PS 1000 be calling a buncha dirty, stinkin' junkyard scavengers like the Second Street Specials, Polly?" Ralph asked, never taking his eyes off of Max.

"Gee, Ralph," snickered Polly the Pigeon, "you don't suppose these fancy school pets need our *help*, do ya?"

Ralph got up real close to Max and said, "Well, fuzzball. *Do ya?*"

"Yes," Max said, pushing Ralph away. "We *do*."

Ralph stood with Polly, Stewart the Squirrel, and his Cockroach Crew.

"So?" Ralph asked. "What is it *this* time?"

"We need a fishing-pole reel," Max explained. "And we need it *pronto*."

"It's gonna cost ya, squirt," said Ralph.

"Just make sure you get it here in an hour, you dirty rat," said Max.

"Dirty?" Ralph snorted. "I took a bath two weeks ago!"

CHAPTER FOUR

"**C**LASS PET SQUAD! TO HEADQUARTERS IMMEDIATELY FOR A STATUS REPORT!"

"What's a 'status report,' Max?" Suzu asked as she bounced into the room.

"It means what everyone's done so far," said Max.

"Well, why didn't you just say *that*?" Suzu asked.

Max smacked his forehead and rolled his eyes.

"I printed a map to Ben's house," Rhonda said. "And came up with the fastest way there."

Max gave Rhonda a short nod of approval and then turned to Julius.

"Okay," said Max. "Your turn."

Julius reached up and pulled down a roll of paper hanging from the ceiling, but it fell off of the spool and onto the floor. Julius scratched his head, looking up at the spool.

"Hmm, my chart seems to have fallen down," he said. "Just give me about an hour or so to repair it and—"

"We don't have time!" Max shouted. "Just get on with it!"

"Very well," Julius said, smoothing out the large sheet of paper.

"As we discussed," said Julius, pointing to a drawing, "we will require a vehicle of some sort in order to transport us to—"

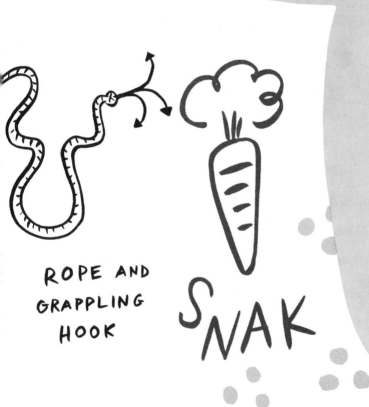

ROPE AND
GRAPPLING
HOOK

SNAK

"Yeah yeah yeah!" Max said impatiently. "The Maestros are already working on that. What *else* do we need?"

"Well, I suggest a grappling hook and a rope to scale walls," said Julius. "And I thought it might be wise to also have a catapult to possibly launch the toy directly into Ben's bedroom window. And—what's *this*?"

"A snack!" Suzu smiled. "We may get hungry!"

Max shook his head and said, "Okay, Squad. Now that we're—"

"Hey!" said Suzu. "What about *me*? Don't you want to know what *I* did?"

"Okay, Suzu," Max sighed. "What did *you* do?"

"I covered Sharkman with glitter!" she said proudly. "Doesn't he look better?"

"Better in what way?" Julius asked, scratching his head.

"He *is* kinda cute now." Rhonda smiled.

"Will you guys get back to work?" Max shouted.

A while later, as Max was in the cafeteria de-glittering Sharkman, he heard something.

"Take a look around, fellas," said Ralph as he and the Second Street Specials were walking up to Max. "This is how the other half lives."

"Fancy!" said Stewart the Squirrel.

"Clean!" said Polly.

"Don't get too used to this place," said Max. "You're *not* a class pet."

"Keep your fur on, pip-squeak," Ralph snickered. "This place ain't our style. We much prefer the junkyard. *Right*, gang?"

The Second Street Specials nodded.

"So?" Max asked. "Did you get it?"

"Have I ever let you down, half-pint?" Ralph asked.

Ralph snapped his fingers and the Cockroach Crew scurried up, carrying a rusty fishing reel. Max looked it over, then nodded.

"It'll have to do," said Max. "What do you want for it?"

"Got any of those fish sticks left?" Stewart asked hopefully.

"Rhonda!" Max shouted, not taking his eyes off of Ralph. "A box of fish sticks for our *friends*."

A few moments later, Rhonda walked up, carrying a box of fish sticks. She put it down next to Max.

"Let's have the reel, rat," said Max.

"Let's have the *sticks*, fuzzball," sneered Ralph.

Max slowly slid the box toward Ralph as Ralph slid the reel toward Max, neither of them taking their eyes off of the other.

Max picked up the reel and handed it to Rhonda.

"Please give this to the Maestros," Max told her.

Ralph snapped his fingers and the Cockroach Crew picked up the box of fish sticks and scurried away.

"Nice doin' business with ya, squirt," Ralph sneered.

As he turned and walked away, Max could hear Stewart say to Ralph, "You should have held out for *two* boxes!"

A while later, the Squad was gathered in the science room.

"Okay, Class Pet Squad!" Joe said. "Get ready to be dazzled!"

"One rope and grappling hook!" Shirley announced as Harry held up a rope made out of paper clips with a pipe cleaner grappling hook at the end of it.

"Show 'em how it works, Harry," Shirley said.

Harry swung the rope in a wide circle and hooked the windowsill with the hook. Then he climbed up the wall and onto the sill. He waved to everyone, but lost his balance and fell back down, hitting his head. He sat up and gave everyone a thumbs-up.

"Is he okay?" Rhonda asked.

"Sure!" said Joe. "That's the fifth time he did that today."

"One catapult!" Joe said, pointing to a contraption made out of a ruler, an eraser, and some thumbtacks.

"Hop on, Harry," Shirley said.

Harry hopped on and Shirley gave Joe the signal. Joe pulled out one of the thumbtacks holding the catapult down.

Sproing!

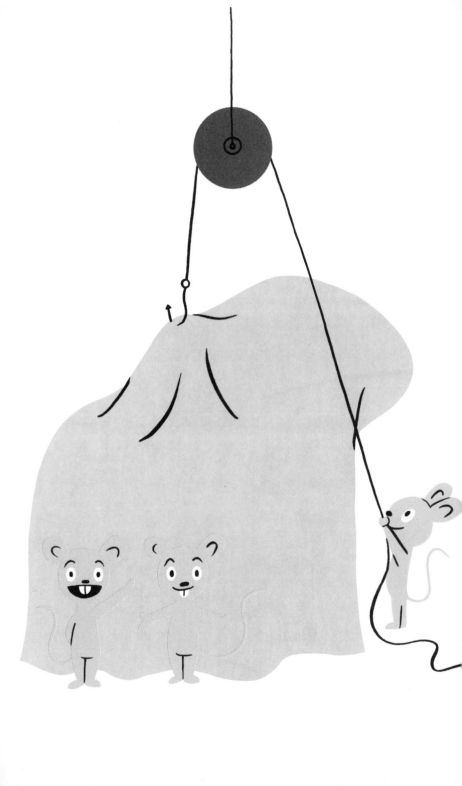

Harry flew into the air and smacked against the wall, then slid down to the floor.

"That's the *sixth* time he did *that* today," Joe explained.

"This is our greatest invention yet!" said Joe.

"You say that every time," said Max.

"Because it's true!" said Joe.

"You asked for a vehicle to get you to Ben's house without anyone noticing it?" Shirley asked. "Well, you got one!"

Harry pulled the towel off.

"May we present the Woof-O-Matic!" Shirley and Joe shouted.

"Let's show them how it works!" said Joe.

The Maestros hopped in and took the controls, then made their invention walk around the room. Harry pumped the fishing reel as the vehicle wobbled and made a funny clanking sound.

"He's cute!" said Rhonda.

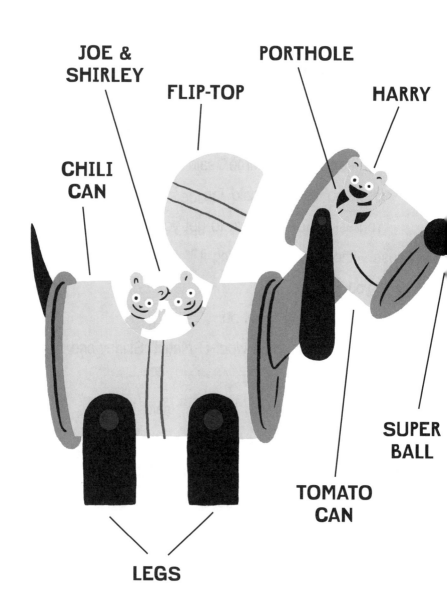

JOE &
SHIRLEY

FLIP-TOP

PORTHOLE

HARRY

CHILI
CAN

SUPER
BALL

TOMATO
CAN

LEGS

"He looks exactly like a real dog!" shouted Suzu.

"I agree," said Julius. "As long as you don't look at it too closely."

"This thing better work," Max grumbled.

"It's guaranteed," said Shirley.

"Or your money back!" said Joe.

CHAPTER FIVE

Max spent the next hour getting the supplies ready and loading up the Woof-O-Matic. Time was running out!

Once they were ready to leave, Max gathered everyone together.

"I'm not going to lie to you, Squad. This is the most dangerous mission we've ever gone on, and we may not all make it back," Max said grimly, pacing back and forth. "You will face peril at every turn!"

They all shuddered.

"But we're here to serve the students of PS 1000!" Max continued, shaking off any fear. "And we *will* successfully complete this mission! Now gather round."

They all came together in a circle and placed their paws and claws on top of each other.

"THE CLASS PET SQUAD
IS ON THE JOB!"

With Sharkman de-glittered and safely loaded, the Class Pet Squad boarded the Woof-O-Matic.

Julius sat in the copilot's seat studying the map to Ben's house, Max took his place at the helm, and Rhonda began cranking the fishing-pole reel, causing the Woof-O-Matic to lurch forward.

"What do *I* do?" Suzu asked, looking around.

"Just sit there, be quiet, and don't touch anything!" Max grunted.

"But—" Suzu said.

"CLASS PET SQUAD MOVING OUT!" Max shouted into a kitchen funnel installed in the dog's mouth as he gripped the steering stick and peered into the viewfinder.

Screech!

Joe lifted an air vent cover and stepped aside.

The Maestros wished them good luck as they watched the Class Pet Squad set off into the night on their most dangerous mission yet.

"Well, well, well," said Ralph. "It looks like those do-gooders are off to um, uh . . ."

"Do good?" Stewart asked.

"*Whatever*," Ralph grumbled. "Pass me a fish stick."

"More power!" Max ordered, peering through the scope as he steered.

"I'm pumping as fast as I can!" Rhonda shouted over the grinding gears.

Julius squinted at the map and then said, "Make a left on Elm Street."

"Right!" said Max.

"Can *I* steer now?" Suzu pleaded.

"No, Suzu!" Max shouted. "What? Make a *right*? Make up your mind!"

Max yanked the stick to the right and the Woof-O-Matic turned, clanking down an alley.

"We're going the wrong way," Julius said, pointing to the map.

Max slammed on the brakes when they came to a brick wall.

"What kind of navigator *are* you, Julius?" Max shouted. "We hit a dead end!"

"I told you to make a *left*," Julius said.

"Well, maybe I couldn't hear you because *some*body was distracting me!" Max said, glaring at Suzu.

"All you guys have jobs," Suzu whimpered, "but I don't."

"You should let her steer, Max," Rhonda said.

"*I'm* the leader of this Squad," said Max, "and *I* decide who does what!"

Then they started shouting and no one could hear each other, but they all fell silent when they heard just one small sound. Max peered into the periscope.

Meow.

Uh-oh.

CHAPTER SIX

Just as Suzu gasped in delight at the sound of a cute, cuddly kitty she could play with, Max, Rhonda, and Julius all clamped their hands over her mouth.

Then they heard the sound of growling, and not just one cat, but *several*.

Max peeked into the scope.

Sure enough, there was a whole gang of alley cats circling the Woof-O-Matic.

Gulp!

"Hey, pooch!" one of the cats said. "We're the Alley Cats and we don't like any mutts invading our turf!"

Rhonda and Julius looked wide-eyed at Max, and waited for his instructions.

He knew that the Woof-O-Matic couldn't move very fast, so a quick retreat was out of the question. And it wouldn't survive a direct assault because it wasn't exactly the sturdiest vehicle.

Max gathered the Squad close and whispered.

"You've been warned, pooch," the cat said. "Now, get ready to be taught a lesson Alley Cat style!"

As the cats moved in, Max, Rhonda, Julius, and Suzu all gathered around the kitchen funnel in the Woof-O-Matic's mouth.

BARK! BARK! BARK!

Max looked through the scope. Not a cat in sight.

Whew!

"Remind me to thank the Maestros for thinking of that feature," Max said to Julius as he pointed to the funnel.

Everyone quickly took their places once more.

"Let's *go*!" Max shouted as he made a wide U-turn and guided the Woof-O-Matic out of the alley and back on track toward Ben's house.

"Can I—?" Suzu started.

"Two more blocks to go, Max," announced Julius.

"Pick up the pace!" Max shouted, so Rhonda pumped harder.

Suzu sighed.

When they finally arrived at Ben's house, Max steered the Woof-O-Matic around to the backyard.

"Okay, Squad," said Max. "We've made it to—"

Grrr!

"That doesn't sound like a cat," Julius observed.

"It sounds a lot *bigger*," Rhonda said nervously.

Max peered through the scope.

Grrrrrrr.

"Abandon ship!" Max shouted as he kicked open the emergency hatch. "Everybody out the stern *now*!"

"Where's the *stern*, Max?" Suzu asked.

"It's in the back!" Max shouted.

"Why didn't you just say *that*?" Suzu asked.

The Squad made it out safely just as the dog clamped down on the Woof-O-Matic with his sharp

fangs. They took refuge inside a hollow garden gnome as they watched the dog tear it to pieces.

"What th—?" the dog said as he examined the pieces of this very strange intruder.

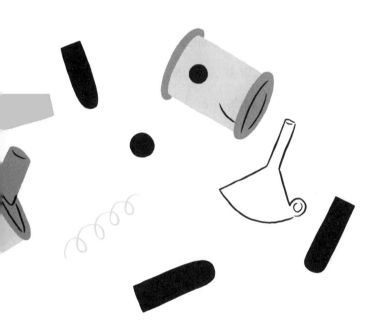

As the dog nosed the twisted cafeteria utensils, gears, and springs, he caught a whiff of something else. Some*one* else.

"Who's there?" he growled. "Show yourself!"

Max motioned for the Squad to stay in the gnome and remain silent and still.

Suddenly, Suzu's nose began to twitch.

"I have to sneeze!" she whispered as she started to get ready to, but they stopped her just in time.

Everyone breathed a sigh of relief. *Whew!*

The dog turned and began to walk away when—

Achoo!

"Sorry!" Suzu squeaked.

Grrr!

CHAPTER SEVEN

"I'm not putting my Squad in danger!" Max said. "I'm going out there to face him."

"That would not be a good idea," Julius said as he held Max back. "That dog is at least ten times your size."

Max ignored Julius's wise advice and bravely bounded toward the dog, his tiny fists raised and ready to fight.

"Come on, Fido! I'm not afraid of you!" Max shouted. "Take your best shot!"

82

"The name's Brutus," the dog growled. "And you're trespassing on my lawn, so—"

But then something caught his eye.

It was Sharkman. And it looked like it was *floating*!

"What th—" Brutus asked.

Rhonda slowly stopped blending into the grass and then everyone could see her.

"Where did you get Ben's toy?" Brutus asked, stepping up to Rhonda and sniffing Sharkman. "And what's that *smell*?"

"It's glitter!" Suzu smiled. "But Max washed it off because he's no fun."

"Please don't eat us," Rhonda pleaded. "We only wanted to give Ben back his toy."

Julius explained that Ben forgot to put Sharkman in his backpack and they traveled all the way from his school to bring it back to him.

Brutus silently looked down at the little strangers and they looked back up, not knowing what the giant dog would do.

"Thank you," Brutus finally said. "That was very kind of you."

The Class Pet Squad heaved a sigh of relief as Brutus apologized for barking at them, but explained that it was his duty to protect and serve the McGillicuttys. Max nodded. He understood completely.

"Come with me," said Brutus. "Ben needs to have all of his toys lined up to fall asleep and his bedtime is soon."

Brutus led them to the dining room window, which faced the backyard. He told the Squad it was

usually open because that's where Ben secretly tossed him his unwanted meatloaf, but he hadn't done that in a while, so maybe it was locked.

Julius managed to recover the rope and grappling hook from the pieces of the shredded Woof-O-Matic and brought them to Max, who swung it around until it caught the windowsill. Then Max scaled the side of the house and hoisted himself up to the window.

"It's *locked*!" Max announced after trying to open it several times.

By the time he climbed back down, Julius was already trying to think of another way to get into

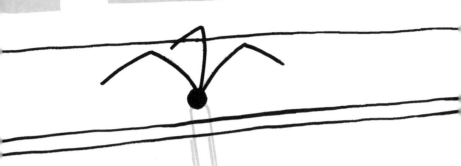

the house. Max, Julius, and Rhonda all argued about what to do.

"Hey—" Suzu said.

"Not *now*, Suzu!" Max barked.

"How about—" Suzu tried to talk.

"Can't you see we're *busy*?" Max snapped.

"But I have an—" Suzu said.

"I said *not now*!" Max growled.

"SANTA CLAUS!" Suzu shouted as loud as she could.

Everyone stopped and looked at her.

"If Santa Claus can use the chimney," Suzu said, "then why can't *we*?"

They all looked at one another, then up at the chimney.

"That's actually not a bad idea, Max," said Julius. "We could catapult you right into the chimney."

"Then, let's do it!" Max shouted, clapping his hands. "Let's go, Squad!"

Within moments, Rhonda and Julius were setting up the catapult and Max was strapping Sharkman to his back, getting ready to be launched into the air and into the chimney.

"Can *I* go, Max?" Suzu asked. *"Please?"*

"No way!" Max said, checking the catapult. "I can't risk you getting injured."

Suzu's shoulders slumped and she sighed, then trudged back to the garden gnome.

"We're almost ready, Max," said Julius as Rhonda readied the catapult.

"Where's Suzu?" Rhonda asked.

"Huh? I don't know," Max grunted. "Over there somewhere."

"She really wanted to be the one to go," Rhonda said. "I think you hurt her feelings, Max."

"Feelings?" Max sputtered. "There's no place for feelings on a dangerous mission!"

"It *was* her idea," Julius reminded him.

"*I'm* the leader of this Squad," said Max, "and *I* decide who does what and—"

Rhonda and Julius just looked at him.

"Oh, all right!" Max groaned and rolled his eyes. "Anything to complete this mission."

Max cleared his throat and awkwardly shifted on his back paws.

"Suzu, um," Max mumbled. "Would *you* like to be the one to go into the house and bring Ben his toy?"

Suzu shrugged.

"Well, isn't that what you *wanted*?" Max asked.

Suzu shrugged again.

"Oh, all right," Max groaned. "I'm sorry I hurt your feelings."

"Yay!" Suzu shouted as she hopped over to Max and gave him a great big hug and a kiss.

Blech! Max pushed her away and quickly composed himself.

"All right, all right," Max sputtered, wiping away her kiss. "Now, can we get back to the mission and get that kid his toy?"

Suzu was already happily hopping to the catapult.

CHAPTER EIGHT

"**N**ow, remember," Max said to Suzu, "put Sharkman in Ben's backpack."

"This is gonna be so cool!" Suzu shouted.

"And make sure no one sees you," Max said.

"I'm gonna fly in the air!" Suzu shouted.

"And then get out of there as fast as possible!" Max said.

"Wahhoo!" Suzu shouted. "Let's *go*!"

"Maybe this wasn't such a good idea," said
Julius.

"You have to hurry!" said Brutus. "Ben's bedtime
is in a few minutes."

"Three, two, one!" Rhonda said as Julius yanked
the thumbtack out of the ground.

Sproing!

"*Whee!*" Suzu shouted as she sailed through the air. "This is *fun*!"

"It's *not* fun!" Max called to her. "It's a dangerous mission!"

Suzu landed safely on the roof and waved to her friends below. Max impatiently motioned for her to go down the chimney.

She climbed up and attached the grappling hook to the side of the chimney just as Max had showed her. Then she lowered herself using the rope and shouting "Ho! Ho! Ho! I'm Santa Claus!" until the

paper clips pulled apart, sending her tumbling down
the chimney and into the living room.

Fortunately, the McGillicuttys had a nice, clean
fireplace.

Max anxiously watched Suzu from the window
and pointed to the stairs that led up to the
bedrooms, but Suzu thought he was waving at her,
so she waved back.

There were so many things for her to see and do inside the house!

She came to a flight of stairs, so she hopped up them. This was *fun*! Suzu soon found herself in

a bedroom, which made her stop and remember
something, but she wasn't exactly sure what it was
she was supposed to remember to remember.

Then she looked at what she was holding—
Sharkman.

She scratched her head until it all came back to
her. She was supposed to put Sharkman in Ben's
backpack. *Right!*

Suzu looked around the bedroom and noticed
that Ben liked unicorns, princesses, and the color
pink! Then she saw a shelf of pretty toys and
wanted to get a better look, so she climbed up the
dresser, but accidentally knocked a few things over.

"Mama?" a small sleepy voice said.

Suzu froze and looked down into a crib in the
corner. Then it hit her—this wasn't Ben's room! It
was his *little sister's* room.

But before she could climb back down to look
for Ben's room, Suzu heard something else: big
footsteps!

"Are you okay, sweetie?" A lady appeared in the
doorway. Suzu stayed as still as possible and didn't
blink.

The little girl sat up and rubbed her eyes. Her mother walked over and tucked her back in, then reached for the shelf Suzu was sitting on with the rest of the toys.

"Here you go," Mrs. McGillicutty said as she placed Suzu next to the little girl, who clutched her close.

Then Mrs. McGillicutty looked down and smiled. Suzu tried her best to remain still and to not blink.

She finally left and Suzu would have heaved a sigh of relief, if the little girl wasn't holding her so tightly.

As Suzu lay there waiting for the girl to fall asleep, she could hear Ben frantically looking for Sharkman in the other room.

"Five minutes until lights out, Ben!" Mrs. McGillicutty called.

"But I can't find Sharkman, Mom!" Ben cried.

Suzu knew she had to get the toy to Ben and fast, but the girl was restless, so Suzu hummed her a lullaby until she finally fell asleep. *Whew!*

Suzu managed to release herself from the girl's sleepy iron grip. She grabbed Sharkman, and then dove into a pile of dirty laundry.

"How many times do I have to tell you to put your dirty laundry in the hamper?" Ben's mom asked, shaking her head.

She scooped up Suzu and the laundry and lifted the lid of the hamper in Ben's room, then dropped it all in.

Thunk!

As Suzu saw Ben leave his room to look for his toy, she hopped out and found his school backpack.

Suzu unzipped it and as she shoved Sharkman in, she noticed Ben's lunchbox. She looked around

and lifted an ear. Ben and his mother were
downstairs, so she opened it.

Carrots!

Suzu chomped on Ben's uneaten carrots and
boy, were they good! Before she could start on the
half-eaten peanut butter and jelly sandwich, she
heard footsteps
climbing the stairs.
She zipped up the
backpack and tried
to hop back to the
hamper, but it was
too late. Ben and
his mother were
already walking
into the room!

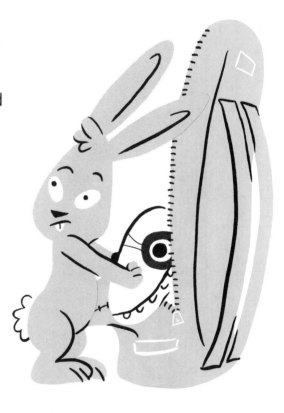

"Just look one
more time, Ben,"
Mrs. McGillicutty
said.

"But I already looked in my backpack!" Ben cried.

At Mrs. McGillicutty's insistence, Ben unzipped his backpack and sure enough, there was Sharkman!

"See? It was right where you left it!" Mrs. McGillicutty said. "Now, put it on your shelf and get to bed!"

Ben placed Sharkman on the shelf and looked at all of his action figures lined up, then smiled.

His mom tucked him in and pulled his lunchbox out of his backpack.

"Oh, good!" she said. "You ate all of your carrots. I'll be sure to give you even more tomorrow."

"Huh?" Ben asked.

"Good night, honey," Mrs. McGillicutty said.

As she walked across the room, she stumbled over Suzu still lying on the floor pretending to be a toy.

"How did this get in *here*?" she asked. She picked Suzu up and walked back to Ben's little sister's room.

Suzu was once again trapped in the little girl's crib.

After another lullaby, Ben's sister was asleep and Suzu was free.

She began to head for the stairs, but decided to peek into Ben's room.

There it was. Sharkman was on Ben's shelf along with all of his other action figures, just the way he liked them.

Suzu smiled as she watched Ben blissfully snoozing.

CHAPTER NINE

When the coast was clear, Suzu hopped back down the stairs and into the kitchen. Max was at the window with an anxious expression. She gave him a thumbs-up.

Suzu was about to climb up onto the kitchen counter to open the window, but she remembered something. She opened the fridge, pulled out a plate of meatloaf, and then tossed it out the window to Brutus, who was waiting below.

Suzu then hopped out of the window and landed on the lawn. Rhonda and Julius congratulated her on a job well done. Max, however, asked her question after question about the details of the mission.

"Is Sharkman exactly where he should be?"

"Is Ben asleep?"

"Did anyone see you?"

"Quit worrying!" Suzu smiled. "Everything went *perfectly!*"

"It looks like our work here is done, Squad," said Max. "Time to move on out."

Finally satisfied, Max gathered them around and they recited in unison:

"Good-bye, Brutus!" Rhonda shouted.

Brutus licked meatloaf off his snout and wagged his tail.

The Woof-O-Matic was in a million pieces. Julius said it would take at least a week to put it back together again.

"We need another way to get home," Max said.

Julius paced back and forth saying *hmm*. They knew Julius was thinking, because he always paced and said *hmm* when he was thinking.

Then he brightened and told the Squad to follow him.

"The garden gnome is hollow, so we can place it over us," Julius explained. "And we can walk back to school without anyone seeing us."

121

"It could work!" said Rhonda.

"It sounds like fun!" said Suzu.

"It'll have to do," said Max.

After traveling for what seemed like hours, Max asked Julius where they were.

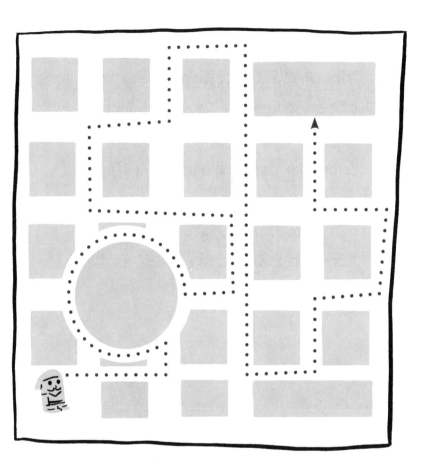

"We're at Thirty-Third Street," Julius said, looking at the map, "and we should arrive at PS 1000 in approximately ten minutes."

They all heaved a sigh of relief.

That is, until they heard a familiar sound.

MEOW.

"Hey, Shorty!" one of the cats said. "We're the Alley Cats and we don't like anybody invading our turf!"

Before Max could come up with a plan, the cat swatted at the gnome, knocking it over and exposing Max, Rhonda, Julius, and Suzu.

"Looky what we have here, fellas!" said the cat. "Dinner for each of us!"

"But, Boss," said another cat, "there's three of us and four of them."

"Then the leftover one will be dessert!" he snickered.

There was no place to run and no place to hide.
This was it.

"It's been an honor serving with you," Max said as the hungry cats slowly approached, licking their lips.

CHAPTER TEN

"**I** wouldn't do that if I were you," a voice called.

"Oh, *yeah*?" the cat asked as he turned around.

A large figure stepped out of the shadows.

"Yeah," said Brutus.

The Squad cheered as the cats ran off.

"Thanks, Brutus!" Rhonda said.

Suzu hugged him.

"Excellent ambush," Max said as he saluted
Brutus. "Good work, sir."

"It was most fortunate that you appeared when you did," said Julius. "But we still need a way to get back to PS 1000."

"Not a problem," Brutus said, kneeling down. "Climb aboard."

"So, how did you find us?" Suzu asked as they trotted back to school.

"That's easy," Brutus said. "I just followed your scent."

"But why did you follow us?" Rhonda asked.

Brutus said he had a hunch they may need his help and he wanted to thank them again.

"Just doing our job," said Max. "A thank you is not necessary."

"But *sometimes* they're nice," Suzu added.

Max looked at Suzu and thought for a moment.

"You're *right*, Suzu," said Max humbly. "Good work. Thank you."

She gasped in delight and gave him a great big hug and a kiss.

Blech! Max pushed her away and quickly composed himself.

"All right, all right," Max sputtered, wiping away her kiss. "A simple 'you're welcome' would've been enough."

The next morning after the second bell rang, the seats were filled and the room was brimming with the chatter of the kids of PS 1000. Max looked out at the classroom and saw Ben McGillicutty.

Max beamed with pride as he watched Ben happily drawing a picture of Sharkman.

Then he thought about the Class Pet Squad's last mission and, sure, it was their most dangerous yet, but it was worth it. Then he looked out at the students. *His* students.

And there was nothing he wouldn't do for each and every one of them.

Thank you for reading this FEIWEL AND FRIENDS book.
The Friends who made

CLASS PET SQUAD

Journey to the Center of Town

possible are:

Jean Feiwel
publisher

Liz Szabla
editor in chief

Rich Deas
senior creative director

Holly West
editor

Dave Barrett
executive managing editor

Raymond Ernesto Colón
senior production manager

Anna Roberto
editor

Christine Barcellona
associate editor

Emily Settle
administrative assistant

Anna Poon
editorial assistant

Follow us on Facebook or visit us online at mackids.com.

OUR BOOKS ARE FRIENDS FOR LIFE

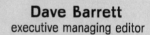